Governing the United States

Ask a Judge

Christy Mihaly

ROurke
Educational Media
rourkeeducationalmedia.com

A Division of
Carson
Dellosa
Education

BEFORE AND DURING READING ACTIVITIES

Before Reading: *Building Background Knowledge and Vocabulary*

Building background knowledge can help children process new information and build upon what they already know. Before reading a book, it is important to tap into what children already know about the topic. This will help them develop their vocabulary and increase their reading comprehension.

Questions and Activities to Build Background Knowledge:

1. Look at the front cover of the book and read the title. What do you think this book will be about?
2. What do you already know about this topic?
3. Take a book walk and skim the pages. Look at the table of contents, photographs, captions, and bold words. Did these text features give you any information or predictions about what you will read in this book?

Vocabulary: *Vocabulary Is Key to Reading Comprehension*

Use the following directions to prompt a conversation about each word.

- Read the vocabulary words.
- What comes to mind when you see each word?
- What do you think each word means?

Vocabulary Words:
- appeals
- appoint
- cases
- civil
- Constitution
- court
- jury
- trials

During Reading: *Reading for Meaning and Understanding*

To achieve deep comprehension of a book, children are encouraged to use close reading strategies. During reading, it is important to have children stop and make connections. These connections result in deeper analysis and understanding of a book.

Close Reading a Text

During reading, have children stop and talk about the following:

- Any confusing parts
- Any unknown words
- Text to text, text to self, text to world connections
- The main idea in each chapter or heading

Encourage children to use context clues to determine the meaning of any unknown words. These strategies will help children learn to analyze the text more thoroughly as they read.

When you are finished reading this book, turn to the next-to-last page for **Text-Dependent Questions** and an **Extension Activity**.

TABLE OF CONTENTS

What a Judge Does 4

Different Kinds of Judges 12

Interesting Things About
Being a Judge 18

Infographic:
Government of the United States 21

Glossary 22

Index...23

Text-Dependent Questions 23

Extension Activity...23

About the Author...24

What a Judge Does

Judges wear black robes. They sit at big desks. What else do judges do? Ask a judge!

What is a judge's job?

Judges work for the government. They work in the judicial branch. Judges hear **cases** in **court**. They decide if somebody broke the law. They can order people to pay money. They can send people to jail. They make sure people are treated fairly.

Some judges run **trials**. At trial, two sides present facts. Each side argues that they are following the law. The judge asks questions. They decide which side is right.

When people do not agree with the judge's decision, they can ask for the case to be heard again. An **appeals** court reviews the case and decides whether or not the trial judge made a mistake.

How does a person become a judge?

There are many ways to become a judge. Many governors **appoint** state judges. In some states, the voters elect judges.

Members of the Florida Supreme Court, shown here, are appointed by the governor.

The United States president picks federal judges. The U.S. Senate reviews the president's choices. It votes to confirm them.

Sandra Day O'Connor is sworn in as the first woman on the U.S. Supreme Court in 1981.

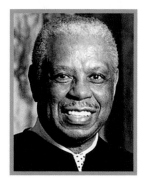

Lifetime Job

Most federal judges are appointed for life. They know their jobs are safe. They don't have to worry about whether their decisions will be popular.

Judge Damon Keith, a champion of civil rights, was a judge for over 50 years!

Who do judges work with?

The judge sits alone at trial. Other people help behind the scenes. The judge's clerks review both sides' arguments. They discuss cases with the judge.

Judges work together on appeals courts. Several judges hear each case. They vote on their decision.

Do judges sit in court all day?

No. Judges study the law. They read. They do research. They write decisions.

Judges may call two sides together to talk. They work to settle cases. If both sides agree, they will not go to trial. The trial will be dismissed.

Different Kinds of Judges

What different courts do judges work on?

There are federal, state, and local courts. Federal courts deal with federal, or national, laws. Most cases involve state laws. Those go to state or local courts. Many cities have local courts.

· UNITED · STATES · COURT · HOUSE ·

Some courts hear only criminal cases. They deal with crimes. Some courts hear **civil** cases. Civil cases involve disagreements between people. A person may bring a civil case to claim money they think they are owed.

Some cases go to special courts. Speeding drivers end up in traffic court. Small claims judges hear arguments over small amounts of money. Family court cases involve parents and children.

Staying Out of Jail
Some people arrested for small crimes don't go to court. They go to community justice centers. These centers help people find jobs. They may help them find doctors. They keep people out of jail.

How do trial judges decide cases?

In some trials, a **jury** is chosen to decide whether someone is guilty or not guilty. The judge explains to the jury how to do their job.

Some cases have no jury. Then, the judge decides the facts. The lawyers explain why the law is on their side. The judge considers the law. They decide which side is right.

What's special about the U.S. Supreme Court?

The U.S. Supreme Court is the highest-ranking court in the country. It decides what the U.S. **Constitution** means. The Constitution is the highest law of the land. Supreme Court Justices have the final say in the nation's court system. They can even decide whether plans proposed by the president are unconstitutional.

The U.S. Supreme Court Building is in Washington, D.C.

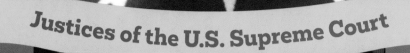

Justices of the U.S. Supreme Court

John Roberts
Chief Justice

Samuel Alito
Associate Justice

Stephen Breyer
Associate Justice

Ruth Bader Ginsburg
Associate Justice

Neil Gorsuch
Associate Justice

Elena Kagan
Associate Justice

Brett Kavanaugh
Associate Justice

Sonia Sotomayor
Associate Justice

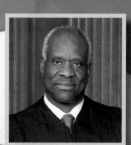

Clarence Thomas
Associate Justice

Interesting Things About Being a Judge

What else can judges do?

A judge can order someone to come into court. They can order a person to stay away from somebody else. They can give police permission to search a house. Judges can also do something more fun. They can conduct weddings!

U.S. Supreme Court Justice Sonia Sotomayor writes children's books about her childhood. Her parents came from Puerto Rico. Her family was poor. She was sick with diabetes. Justice Sotomayor always wanted to make the world better, and she says anyone can do this.

Judges make sure people follow the law. They protect people's rights. That's important work!

Government of the United States

	Legislative Branch Makes the laws.	Executive Branch Carries out the laws.	Judicial Branch Decides what laws mean.
Federal Governs the whole country.	**Congress** Includes Senators and members of the House of Representatives.	**The President** Works with cabinet members such as the U.S. Attorney General.	**U.S. Courts** Judges work at many courts, including the U.S. Supreme Court.
State Governs each of the 50 states.	**State Legislature** Representatives work at the capitol building in each state's capital city.	**The Governor** Works with many officials such as the Secretary of State and the State Attorney General.	**State Courts** Include the highest court in the state—the state Supreme Court.
Local Governs each village, town, or city.	**City Council** Representatives make rules about how land is used, where roads will be built, and more.	**The City Mayor** Is in charge of the police department, the parks department, and more.	**Local Courts** Judges rule on cases that involve city laws and crimes that are less serious.

Glossary

appeals (uh-PEELZ): related to courts that review a lower court's decision

appoint (uh-POINT): to choose someone for a specific job or position

cases (KAY-sez): matters brought to a court of law

civil (SIV-uhl): relating to law cases between people, not involving crimes

Constitution (kahn-sti-TOO-shuhn): the written document that contains the highest law of the United States

court (kort): a place where law cases are heard and decided

jury (JOOR-ee): a group of people (usually 12) who listen to the evidence at a trial and then decide the facts, including whether or not someone accused of a crime is guilty

trials (TRYE-uhlz): court proceedings to hear evidence and decide disputed questions

Index

clerks 8

criminal 13

family court 13

jail 4, 13

Keith, Damon 7

Sotomayor, Sonia 17, 19

Supreme Court 6, 16, 17, 19

voters 6

Text-Dependent Questions

1. What are some powers that judges have?

2. What does an appeals court do, and why do we have them?

3. What does a jury do?

4. Name three different kinds of courts and what they do.

5. Why are federal judges appointed for life?

Extension Activity

What is your state's highest court? Look it up in the library or on your state website. Read about a case that your state high court decided recently. What did each side argue in that case? Write about whether you agree or disagree with the court's decision.

ABOUT THE AUTHOR

Long ago, Christy Mihaly worked as a clerk for the Chief Justice of the California Supreme Court. Later, she spent many years arguing cases as a lawyer. She has degrees in law and policy studies. She is the author of many books, including *Free for You and Me*, a picture book about the First Amendment to the U.S. Constitution. Find out more or say hello at her website: www.christymihaly.com.

www.rourkeeducationalmedia.com

PHOTO CREDITS: cover: ©Jon Bilous; page 4: ©dcdebs; page 5: ©Richlegg; page 6: ©State of Florida; page 7: ©Wiki; page 8: ©filadendron; page 9: ©MR Yanukit; page 10: ©PeopleImages; page 11: ©Mind and I; page 12: ©palinchakjr page 13: ©seb_ra; page 14: ©IPGGutenbergUKLtd; page 15: ©Deborah Cheramie; page 16: ©OrphanCam; page 17a, 17f, 17h, 17i, 19: ©Steve Petteway; page 17b: ©Samuel Alito; page 17c: ©Stephen Breyer; page 17d, 17g: ©Collection of the Supreme Court; page 17e: ©Franz Jantzen; page 18: ©Leonrad Ortiz; page 20: ©Chris Ryan

Edited by: Madison Capitano
Cover design by: Rhea Magaro-Wallace
Interior design by: Janine Fisher

Library of Congress PCN Data

Ask a Judge / Christy Mihaly (Governing the United States)
ISBN 978-1-73162-917-3 (hard cover)
ISBN 978-1-73162-916-6 (soft cover)
ISBN 978-1-73162-918-0 (e-Book)
ISBN 978-1-73163-351-4 (ePub)
Library of Congress Control Number: 2019944966

Rourke Educational Media
Printed in the United States of America,
North Mankato, Minnesota